The Carnival of the Animals

Cover design by Bill Toth.

Book design by Iris Bass.

Cover art: Upper print of a parrot's claw, "Baraboo," courtesy of Teri Henry; middle print of a dog's paw, "Princess Schopenhauer," courtesy of Pat, Don, and Gwen Munson; and bottom print of a cat's paw, "Mischa," courtesy of Iris Bass.

Author photograph by Stephen Fischer.

The Carnival of the Animals

MOACYR SCLIAR

Translated by
Eloah F. Giacomelli

AVAILABLE
PRESS

BALLANTINE BOOKS • NEW YORK

An Available Press Book

Translation Copyright © 1985 by Eloah F. Giacomelli

Library of Congress Catalog Card Number: 85-90507

ISBN 0-345-32853-1

Manufactured in the United States of America

First Edition: January 1986

THE LIONS

Not nowadays, but years ago, lions posed a threat. Thousands, nay, millions of them used to roam Africa, making the jungle quiver with their roars. It was feared that they would invade Europe and America. Wright, Friedman, Mason, and others warned against this possible danger. Consequently, it was decided to wipe out the frightful feline beasts. Their destruction was carried out in the following manner:

A great mass of them, gathered near Lake Chad, was destroyed by one single atom device of medium explosive force dropped from a bomber one summer day. After the characteristic mushroom cloud disappeared, it was ascertained by means of photographs that the nucleus of the leonine mass had been completely disintegrated, and was now surrounded by a two-kilometer-wide band that was strewn with chunks of bloody flesh, fragments of bone, and bloodstained manes. Dying lions lay on its periphery.

The authorities in charge described the operation as "satisfactory." However, as always happens in undertakings of this scope, the residual problems became in turn a source of concern. There was, for instance, the matter of the radioactive lions that had survived the blast and were now roaming the forests. True, about 20 percent of them were killed by the Zulus during the two weeks following the explosion. However, the proportion of casualties among the natives (two for each lion) discouraged even the most optimistic among the experts.

It became necessary to resort to more elaborate methods. For this purpose, a laboratory was set up to train gazelles; the lab's primary goal was to free the animals from their normal instincts. It would be too tiresome to go into the details of this project, which was, incidentally, quite refined; suffice it to say that the method employed—a kind of brainwashing technique adapted to animals—was one devised by Walsh and his assistants. After obtaining a considerable number of these prepared gazelles, they injected them with a powerful dose of a toxic with delayed action. The gazelles then searched out the lions, and let themselves be killed and eaten by them; the beasts of prey, after eating the poisoned flesh, died painlessly within a few days.

The solution seemed ideal; however, there was one race of lions (fortunately, not many of them) that seemed to be resistant to this and other powerful poisons. The task of killing them was assigned to hunters equipped with sophisticated and ultrasecret weapons. This time, only one specimen survived, a female that was captured and quartered near Brazzaville. In the uterus of this lioness, they found a viable fetus: Showing no signs of radioactivity, the tiny animal was raised in an incubator. It was hoped that in this way the exotic fauna would be kept from extinction.

Later the cub was taken to the London Zoo, where despite the tight security, it was killed by a fanatic. The death of the small beast was greeted enthusiastically by large segments of the population. "The lions are dead!" a drunken soldier kept shouting. "From now on everybody will be happy!"

On the following day the Korean War broke out.

THE SHE-BEARS

Prophet Elisha is on his way to Bethel. It is a hot day. Insects are buzzing in the thicket. The prophet is marching at a fast pace. He has an important mission in Bethel.

Suddenly, a large number of children begin to give chase, shouting: "Let's see you levitate, baldy! Come on, levitate!"

Elisha turns around and curses them in the name of the Lord; a moment later, two big she-bears come out of the thicket and devour forty-two kids: The smaller bear devours twelve; the bigger one, thirty.

The little bear has active digestion; the children that fall into its stomach are attacked by powerful acids, made soluble and reduced to small particles. They vanish.

The other thirty children meet with a different fate. Going down the great bear's esophagus, they land in its huge stomach. There they remain. At first, numbed by fear, they cling to one another, barely able to breathe; then the younger kids start to cry and wail, and their cries echo dismally in the large space. "Woe to us! Woe to us!"

Finally, the oldest child turns on a light and they find them-

3

selves in a place resembling a cavern, from whose sinuous walls
a viscous fluid oozes. The ground is strewn with the half-
rotten residue of former prey: babies' skulls, little girls' legs. "Woe
to us!" they wail. "We'll die!"

Time goes by, and seeing that they haven't died, they take heart.
They chat, laugh, play, romp about, throw debris and remains
of food at one another.

When tired out, they sit down and talk in earnest. They orga-
nize themselves and outline a plan of action.

Times goes by. They grow up, but not much; the confined
space doesn't allow for much growth. They are turned into a
strange race of dwarfs, with short limbs and large heads on which
glow beaconlike eyes that endlessly scrutinize the darkness of
the entrails. And there they build their minitown, with pretty white-
washed minihouses. The minischool.

The minitown hall. The minihospital. And they are happy.

They have now forgotten the past. Vague memories still remain, memories that acquire mystic configurations as time goes
by.

They pray: "Great Bears who art in heaven . . ." They appoint
a priest—the Great Prophet, a man with a shaved head and
frightful eyes; once a year he scourges the inhabitants with the
Sacred Whip. He demands faith and hard work. The people,
diligent workers, don't fail him. The ministorehouses overflow
with foodstuffs; the minifactories manufacture thousands of beautiful minithings.

Time goes by. A new generation emerges. After years of hap-
piness, the inhabitants are now worried: Due to some strange
atavism, the children are born with long arms and legs, well-
proportioned heads, and gentle brown eyes. Each birth brings
renewed uneasiness. People begin to grumble: "If they grow much
taller, there won't be room for us." Birth control measures are
under consideration. The minigovernment considers consulting
the Great Prophet about the desirability of executing babies as
soon as they are born. Endless discussions follow.

Time goes by. The children have grown up and they look powerful as they move about in groups. Much bigger than their
parents, it's impossible to restrain them. They take over the

minimovie theaters, the minichurches, the miniclubs. They show
no respect for the police. They roam the minihighways.

One day the Great Prophet is on his way to his minimansion
when the youngsters catch sight of him. Immediately they give
chase, shouting: "Let's see you levitate, baldy! Come on, levitate!"

The prophet turns around and curses them in the name of the
Lord.

Soon afterward two she-bears appear and devour the children—
all forty-two of them.

Twelve are swallowed by the little bear and destroyed. But thirty
go down the esophagus of the great bear and land in its stomach—
a great hollow where the blackest darkness prevails. And there
they remain, crying and wailing: "Woe to us!"

Finally, they turn on a light.

RABBITS

THE RABBIT IS AN ANIMAL THAT IS QUICK AT COPULATING. ALICE opened her eyes. She recalled a story her husband used to tell: about a he-rabbit, who after having relations with a she-rabbit, said to her: "It is very good, my darling—wasn't it?"

She yawned and jumped out of bed. "What's the day today? Wednesday? No, yesterday was Wednesday ... It's the day when we play cards. But did we play cards yesterday? Yes, we did.

"I remember Gilda saying to me—you're lucky—and I was. Wait now, that was Wednesday last week. Or last month?"

She sat down at the dressing table and began to brush her hair. "I'm now brushing my hair. Just as I did yesterday." She looked closely at herself. "My face, always the same. I'm thirty-two years old. I could be twenty-two. Or twelve?" "My little girl." She turned around. There was nobody in the room. However, she had heard her husband's deep voice quite distinctly. She looked at the watch: seven-thirty. At this hour he would be on the highway. He was the manager of a cannery located thirty kilometers outside the city. He owned a big car; an old black Dodge. She would tease him: "Nobody else has such an old car!" "I

7

know, my darling. But the manager of a cannery has to be con-
servative." The laughter, short and coarse. She winced and turned
around again. The wind was stirring the curtains gently. She rose
to her feet and walked to the window.

They lived on the top of a bleak, rocky hill on the outskirts of
the city. It was a beautiful, spacious house, built of solid white
stone and dark wood. The church towers could be seen from there.
"But it's so isolated," she had complained to her husband. "I
know, my darling." A strong man, with thick black eyebrows
and powerful teeth.

A lonely wolf. He would hold her tight in his hairy arms. They
spent the winter evenings sitting before the fireplace. He would
gaze at her in silence. Suddenly, he would say: "The rabbit, my
darling, is an animal that is quick at copulating ..." He would
laugh, hugging her.

She winced.

She drew the curtains aside. A mist, like a white sea, covered
everything. Not even the church towers were visible. The house
floated, half submerged in the fog. A chilly breeze gave her goose
bumps. She closed the window. "How cold it is! I'll put on the
white woolen dress."

She went to the closet and opened the heavy doors, made of
dark cedar. She looked at herself in the mirror. "I'm quite
pretty," she murmured. She was thirty-two years old; she could
be twenty.

Always well-dressed: In a white ...

She was startled: She already had the dress on. "I must be very
absentminded. I got dressed without realizing I was doing so."
Her husband liked the white dress. "You look twelve years old."
They would sit face to face before the fireplace, where a fire
burned. Spellbound, she would sit staring at his teeth, which
glinted in the light of the fire. He would break into his short,
coarse laughter. "The rabbit ..." She would blush. "Why?" he
would ask. "It's this loneliness. I don't like this house, so se-
cluded ..." Saying nothing, he would gaze at her.

But one evening they got into the car, the big black Dodge.
"It's a surprise," he said, laughing. And so it was: They were
going to visit her husband's partner. "Let me introduce you to

my partner, my darling. Rabbit, meet my wife." Rabbit! She
laughed. Everybody was laughing. They played cards on Wednes-
days. The two of them, Rabbit and Gilda.

It felt good to be together ... "The rabbit is an animal that is
quick at copulating ..." She would say and they laughed. It
felt good throughout those sweet winter mornings. "You are an
animal that is quick at copulating." Rabbit would laugh. "White
becomes you, it really does."

Fully dressed, she walked down the grand stairway. She called
the maid: "Julia!" There was no reply. She frowned. Then she
remembered: "Today's Thursday. She must have gone to the market." She was startled: "But is today Thursday? Yes, it must
be. We played cards yesterday, I know! I remember Gilda telling me ... But was it yesterday ... ? It was: I turned thirty-
two on Tuesday. Or was it twenty-two?" Her husband had
promised her a present.

The big table had been set—for one person. She always had
coffee by herself in the huge dining room. It displeased her
greatly—this solitude. She sat down.

"I'm going to the hairdresser ... But is this the day when I
always have an appointment with the hairdresser?" She took
the coffeepot, then checked herself: Her cup was already filled
with coffee. "Who poured it? Did I? Strange, isn't it—wasn't
it?"

She put the coffeepot down, and stood motionless, absolutely
still.

It was only a few minutes later that she saw the white rabbit.

Her hand reached out abruptly, overturning the cup.

A black coffee stain spread over the white tablecloth. Behind
the coffeepot, a white plush bunny.

"For my second birthday my father gave me a white plush
bunny." Alice and her white rabbit, he said laughing. The white
teeth, the bushy eyebrows. "When I was two years old. Or when
I was twelve?"

She was crying. She rose from the table. "But today's Thursday! We're getting together at eight o'clock!" Sweet winter
mornings. Sweet kisses. She was laughing.

She dashed out to the garage and took out the small white

car, a present from her husband. On the front seat—a white plush rabbit. Her eyes were blurred with tears as she began to go down the narrow, gravelly road. "It's late! It's late!" The fog was getting denser and denser.

"Wait for me, Rabbit!" She was running. "The rabbit is an animal . . ." Her husband was laughing.

It was then that she saw the big black Dodge looming large before her. Her husband, his fingers gripping the steering wheel, was laughing—baring his powerful teeth, which were white, very white. Shards of glass piercing her throat, a mass of metal crushing her chest.

Everything is much too quick—wasn't it? she murmured and closed her eyes.

THE COW

DURING A STORMY NIGHT THERE WAS A SHIPWRECK OFF THE AFrican coast. The ship split in half and sank in less than a minute. Passengers and crew died instantly. There was one survivor, a sailor who had been hurled far away when the disaster occurred. Almost drowning—for he wasn't a good swimmer—the sailor was praying and saying farewell to life, when he saw Carola, the cow, swimming quickly and vigorously next to him.

Carola, the cow, had been loaded in Amsterdam.

A superb breeder, her destination had been a farm in South America.

Holding on to the cow's horn, the sailor let her lead him; and so, at daybreak they reached a sandy islet, where the cow deposited the unfortunate young man, and she kept licking his face until he woke up.

Realizing that he was on a deserted island, the sailor burst into tears. "Woe to me! This island isn't on any sea route! I'll never see another human being again." Throwing himself upon the sand, he cried for a long time, while Carola, the cow, stood gazing at him with her big brown eyes.

Finally, the young man wiped his tears and rose to his feet.

He looked around him: There was nothing on the island except for sharp rocks and a few rickety-looking trees. He felt hungry; he called the cow: "Come here, Carola!" He milked her and drank the good, warm, foamy milk. Then he felt better; he sat down and stood staring at the ocean. "Woe to me!" he would wail at times, but now without much conviction: The milk had done him good.

That night he slept snuggled against the cow. He had a good night's sleep, full of refreshing dreams, and when he woke up, there within his reach was the udder with its abundant milk.

The days went by and the young man grew more and more attached to the cow. "Come here, Carola!" She would obey him.

He would slice off a piece of her tender meat—he was quite partial to tongue—and would eat it raw while still warm, the blood dribbling down his chin. The cow didn't even moo. She merely licked her wounds. The sailor was careful not to injure her vital organs; if he removed a lung, he'd leave the other one in place; he ate the spleen but not the heart, and so on.

With scraps of her skin the sailor made clothes and shoes and a tent to shelter him from the sun and the rain. He cut off Carola's tail and used it to drive the flies away.

When the meat began to get scarce, he hitched the cow to a plow crudely made of tree branches, and then tilled the plot of land lying between the trees, where the soil was more fertile.

He used the animal's excrement for manure. As there wasn't much of it, he ground a few of her bones to powder so that he could use them as fertilizer.

Then he sowed the few grains of corn that had remained stuck in the cavities of Carola's teeth. Soon, seedlings began to sprout and the young man's hopes rekindled.

He celebrated St. John's Day by eating *canjica,* the traditional grated corn pudding.

Spring arrived. At night, from faroff regions, a gentle breeze brought subtle aromas.

Gazing at the stars, the sailor would sigh. One night he plucked out one of Carola's eyes, mixed it with seawater and then swallowed this light concoction. He had voluptuous visions, never before experienced by a human being ... Overcome by desire, he went up to the cow. And in this matter too, Carola was ready to oblige.

A long time went by, and one day the sailor spotted a ship on the horizon. Wild with joy, he began to yell at the top of his voice, but he got no reply: The vessel was much too far away. The sailor plucked out one of Carola's horns and used it as a makeshift trumpet. The powerful sound roared through the air, but even so he failed to make himself heard.

The young man grew desperate: Night was falling and the ship was sailing farther away from the island. At last, the young man set Carola on the ground and threw a lit match into her ulcerated womb, where a scrap of fat still remained.

The cow caught fire quickly. From amid the black smoke, her one remaining eye looked steadily at the sailor. The young man started; he thought he had detected a tear. But it was just an impression.

The huge flash of light called the attention of the captain of the ship; a motorboat came to pick up the sailor. They were about to leave, taking advantage of the tide, when the young man shouted: "Just a minute!" He went back to the island, and from the smoldering pile he took a handful of ashes and put it in his leather vest. "Farewell, Carola," he murmured. The crew of the motorboat exchanged glances. "Sunstricken," one of them said.

The sailor arrived in his native country. He resigned from the sea and became a wealthy and respected farmer who owned a dairy farm with hundreds of cows.

But even so he led a lonely, unhappy life, and he had frightening nightmares every night until he was forty years old. When he turned forty, he traveled to Europe by boat.

One night, unable to sleep, he left his luxurious stateroom and went up to the quarterdeck, which was bathed in moonlight. He lit a cigarette, leaned on the ship's rail, and stood gazing at the sea.

Suddenly he stretched his neck eagerly. He had spotted an islet on the horizon.

"Hi, there!" said someone next to him.

He turned. She was a beautiful blonde with brown eyes and a luxuriant bust.

"My name is Carola," she said.

THE DOG

"Look what I've brought back from my trip," Senhor Armando said to his friend Heitor, taking something out of his pocket. They were sitting in the pleasant front garden of Senhor Heitor's house.

It was a dog; a tiny dog, perhaps the smallest dog in the world. Senhor Armando placed it on the table, where the tiny creature stood throbbing. It was smaller than a whiskey glass.

"What is it?" asked Senhor Heitor.

"It's a Japanese dog. As you know, the Japanese are experts in miniature art. This dog is a typical example. For several generations now they've been crossbreeding ever smaller specimens until they've come up with this tiny creature. And mind you, they started with the wild dog, which is the wolf's next of kin.

"It has retained the ferocity of the wolf," Senhor Armando went on, "now allied with the attributes of the watchdog. In addition, it has undergone several technical improvements. Its teeth have been capped with platinum; they are hard and extremely sharp. In its ears, as you can see, an acoustic device has been implanted to improve its hearing. Over its eyes there are contact

15

lenses that have been specially treated to enable it to see in the dark. And the conditioning! Ah, the conditioning! For twelve years ..."

"Is this animal twelve years old?"

"Twelve, yes. Twelve years of continuous conditioning. It's able to smell out derelicts who are still miles away. It hates their guts. Let me tell you, I feel much more relaxed now that I have this treasure at home with me."

He leaned back in the armchair and took a sip of whiskey.

Just then somebody knocked at the gate. It was a man; a beggar dressed in rags, leaning on a crutch.

"What do you want?" shouted Senhor Heitor.

"A little something for the love of God ..."

"Adolfo!" Senhor Heitor was calling his manservant. "Come here!"

"Just a moment, Heitor," said Senhor Armando, his eyes sparkling. "How would you like to see my little dog in action?" And without waiting for a reply, he whispered into the dog's ear: "Go, Bilbo, go! Bring him here!" And to his friend, "It's the first time he'll be working here in Brazil."

In the meantime, Bilbo had jumped off the table and was darting across the lawn. A moment later, the beggar was walking through the gate as if he were being hauled in by a tractor.

"Did you see that?" Senhor Armando cried out excitedly. And the beggar already stood in front of them, with Bilbo's platinum teeth sunk into the man's only leg.

"What do you want?" demanded Senhor Heitor in a hard tone of voice.

"A little something for the love of ..." the beggar began, his face contorted with pain.

"And why aren't you working, my good man?"

"I can't ... I have only one leg ..."

"There are plenty of jobs which people can do even without a leg."

"I can make more money by begging than by having a job."

"You're a bum!" shouted Senhor Heitor, incensed. "A derelict! The scum of society! Get out of my sight before I punish you."

"Just a moment, Heitor," said Senhor Armando. "Bilbo is pointing out the right course of action to us. Why let this man go free? So that tomorrow he can break into my house, or into yours?"

"But . . ." Senhor Heitor began to say.

"Let's leave this matter for Bilbo to handle. Go, Bilbo, go!"

With a skillful maneuver of its tiny head, Bilbo threw its prey upon the ground. Then, starting with the leg into which its teeth were already sunk, Bilbo began to chew methodically. First, it ate the lower limb; then the stump of the leg; from there it proceeded to the abdomen, the thorax, and the head. Everything happened in a twinkling; simultaneously, the dog sucked up the blood so as not to let it stain the green grass. Finally, the beggar's last remaining part—his right eye—disappeared, still glowing with terror, into the tiny dog's mouth. To finish everything off, Bilbo ate up the crutch that had been left leaning against the table.

"Did you see that?" said Senhor Armando, pleased. "Even the wood."

"Very ingenious," remarked Senhor Heitor, taking a sip of whiskey. "I'll accept it."

"What do you mean?" Senhor Armando was astonished.

"In exchange for the money you owe me."

"No way, Heitor!" shouted Senhor Armando indignantly. He rose to his feet, picked up the tiny dog and placed it in his pocket. "A debt is a debt. You'll get your money when it is due. You can't put a money value on this dog. Your attitude surprises me. I never suspected a gentleman could act in such a way. Good-bye!"

He headed for the gate.

"You derelict!" shouted Senhor Heitor. "You thief!"

Senhor Armando turned around. He was about to say something but instead let out a howl. Senhor Heitor, whose eyesight was poor, was looking for his glasses; meanwhile, he could indistinctly see the figure of Senhor Armando disintegrating by the gate. When he finally succeeded in locating his glasses, he saw Bilbo before him, barking joyfully. There were no traces of Senhor Armando.

"Great!" murmured Senhor Heitor, draining off the glass of whiskey.

"Heitor!" It was his wife, who had just appeared at the door. Senhor Heitor quickly put Bilbo in his pocket. "What's that you've got there?"

"It's a . . . a tiny dog," replied Senhor Heitor.

"Well, really, Heitor!" His wife was furious. "How many times have I told you I don't want any animals in this house? Where did you get this dog?"

"From Armando, it was his. He . . . he gave it to me."

"That's a lie! Armando would never give anything to anyone. You stole it from him." The woman's eyes were glowing. "You thief! You derelict!"

Senhor Heitor stood smiling. Suddenly, he let out a howl and vanished. As for the woman, she could see nothing but a tiny dog, its tongue hanging out.

SHAZAM

Comic strips are being reappraised; there has been a lot of talk about the strength of the heroes, yet what is there to be said about their sorrows?

The Invisible Man suffered from a deep feeling of depersonalization. "I keep touching myself all the time to make sure that I'm really present in the world right now," he wrote in his journal. The Rubber Man would buy a suit on one day only to find on the following day that it no longer fit him. He, not the suit, had either shrunk or stretched. Prince Sub-Mariner grieved over the pollution of the sea. And what a temptation, those savory baits! Luckily, he knew fishermen and fishhooks quite well. The Human Torch was constantly being persecuted by sadists carrying fire extinguishers as well as constantly harassed by the fire insurance companies (woe to him if he was caught anywhere near a fire!). The Shadow, who knew all about the evil that lurks in the hearts of men, was vexed by hypochondriacs obsessed about heart diseases. Zorro kept receiving indecent propositions from a fetishist with a fixation on objects beginning with the letter Z.

Lothar was accused of conspiring against the government of one of the fledgling African republics. It was impossible for

anyone to give Superman a shot in the arm; the needles would
break against his steel skin. "One day I'll die because of this,"
he would complain, but nobody paid any attention to what he
said; it has been proved that heroes are impervious to the rav-
ages of time.

—A. Napp, *The Heroes Revisited*

CRIME HAVING BEEN ELIMINATED FROM THE WORLD, CAPTAIN
Marvel was invited to a special session of the American
Congress. There he was greeted by Lester Brainerd, a Louisiana
senator, and awarded the Military Merit Medal and a life pen-
sion. Deeply moved, Captain Marvel expressed his thanks and
stated his desire to live peacefully forever—writing his memoirs,
perhaps.

For his retreat, Captain Marvel selected the city of Pôrto Alegre in Brazil, where he rented a room in a picturesque residential hotel in the Alto da Bronze area.

At first, his life was far from peaceful; whenever he was on
the street, crowds of kids would run after him: "Fly! Fly!" They
would throw stones and make faces at him. Annoyed, Captain
Marvel considered moving to Nepal. As time went by, however, people gradually took less notice of him. He started by giving up his eye-catching attire and now wore ordinary clothes, a
gray Tergal suit. Then, when television started to show a new
movie series, the young people were taken up with the new
heroes that had replaced him. There was a brief moment of glory
when his memoirs were launched at an autograph party attended by dozens of people. The event received a great deal of
attention and critics saw in his book unexpected values ("A new
outlook on the world," somebody said), but afterward Captain
Marvel was once more forgotten. He spent the days in his room,
leafing through old comic books and nostalgically remembering
the evil Silvana, who had died of cancer many years before.
Sometimes Captain Marvel worked in his garden. He had succeeded in persuading his landlady to let him use the yard beyond
the kitchen, and there he grew roses. He wanted to produce a
hybrid variety.

In the evenings Captain Marvel watched television or went to the movies. With melancholy contempt he watched the modern heroes, unable to fly, vulnerable to bullets, and even so, incredibly violent. He used to spend Saturdays at a bar near the residential hotel, drinking rum with passion fruit juice and chatting with ex-boxers, who had gotten used to his heavy accent.

On one of those evenings Captain Marvel was feeling particularly depressed. He had already had eleven drinks and was thinking of going to bed, when a woman came to the bar, sat down at the counter and asked for a beer.

Silently, Captain Marvel looked her over. He had never paid much attention to women; the fight against crime had always been an engrossing task. But now, being retired, Captain Marvel could afford to think of himself. His peeling mirror revealed that he still cut a splendidly virile figure, and he couldn't help being aware of the fact.

As for the woman, she wasn't pretty. Fortyish, short and fat, she smacked her lips every time she took a gulp of beer. But she was only woman at the bar that Saturday night. Besides, she not only returned the captain's gaze, but also got up, walked over and sat down next to him.

Captain Marvel introduced himself, saying his name was José Silva, a car salesman. He did so feeling ill at ease: Unlike the modern heroes, he wasn't used to dissembling, scheming, disguising himself.

"Shall we go to my room, honey?" the woman whispered at three o'clock in the morning.

They went. It was on the fourth floor of an old building on Rua Duque de Caxias. The wooden steps creaked under their weight. The woman was panting and had to stop at each landing. "It's my blood pressure." Uneasy, Captain Marvel felt like taking her in his arms and flying up; but he didn't want to reveal his identity. Finally, they got there.

The women opened the door. It was a filthy little room, decorated with paper flowers and religious statues. In the corner, a bed covered with a red spread.

The woman drew closer. She turned to Captain Marvel and smiled: "Kiss me, darling." They kissed for a long time, took off their clothes and got into bed. "How cold you are, honey," the woman complained. It was his steel skin—the invulnerable shell that had so often protected Captain Marvel and that was now getting somewhat rusty under the armpits. Captain Marvel thought of rubbing his chest with his hands, but he was afraid that this would create sparks and cause a fire. So he confined himself to saying: "It'll be better soon."

"It's all right. Come now," the woman murmured, her eyes glowing in the dark. Captain Marvel threw himself upon her.

A howl of pain shook the room.

"You've killed me! You've killed me! How it hurts!"

Scared, Captain Marvel turned on the light. The bed was soaked with blood.

"You've stuck a sword into me, you bastard, you devil!"

Hurriedly, Captain Marvel put on his pants. The woman was screaming for help. Not knowing what to do, Captain Marvel opened the window. Lights began to go on in the nearby houses. He jumped.

For a moment he was going down like a stone; but he quickly gained control and glided gently. He flew aimlessly over the city, which was still lying asleep. At times he sobbed; he remembered the days when he was just Billy Batson, a simple radio announcer.

There was one word that could have taken him back to those days; however, Captain Marvel no longer remembered it.

THE FISHING TOURNAMENT

AN EXTREMELY UNPLEASANT INCIDENT TOOK PLACE DURING THE last fishing tournament on Joy Beach.

Outstanding individuals participated in that popular sport.

Among others, the following were present: Miller, Saraiva, Zeca, Judge of the Court of Appeal Otávio, Brunneleschi, and Senhora Santos.

The weather was wonderful. The water abounded in fish.

All one had to do was throw in a fishhook in order to catch a beautiful specimen.

Contentment was widespread. In an atmosphere of goodwill, people congratulated the luckiest among them.

On the third day of the tournament a strange vehicle arrived. It was a large, gaudily painted wagon, pulled by ridiculous-looking jades. Amid a great rumpus, a big clan made up of father, mother, and many children alighted.

As one might have expected, the people already there felt very ill at ease. The newcomers were filthy, rude, and undesirable companions.

The man was especially unpleasant: short, with bronze-colored skin, evil black eyes, a thick-lipped mouth displaying gold-capped teeth. And a vicious tongue: He wouldn't walk past a woman, whether married or single, without uttering a coarse joke.

Had the intruders remained in the empty lot they had chosen for their stopping place, their insolence would have been bearable.

However, on the following morning the man—his name was Antonio—shows up on the beach, and without asking for permission, becomes absorbed in the following activities: He rolls his trouser legs up to his knees. He enters the water, marching right in among the sportsmen's fishing lines. He dips his arms into the water up to his elbows. He utters some words in a low voice. And when he removes his arms, they are filled with fish!

Such violation of the rules caused great uneasiness. The tournament participants complained to the president of the fishing club, who—together with a committee—headed for the parking lot where the weird individuals were camped.

The family was eating lunch. They picked up the fish—some still alive—and put them in their mouths, chewing ravenously. The president alleged that it was against the law to eat the little creatures before they had been weighed and properly registered.

"Know do you what? Want you do what?" Antonio yelled at them in his twisted manner of speech, a morsel of fish intestines hanging out of his lecherous-looking mouth. And with great disrespect, the whole tribe burst out laughing. The president and his committee left, ready to report the affair to the proper authority. However, when the judge of the Court of Appeal heard about the case, he said: "Gentlemen, please leave the matter in my hands."

It was obvious that he was overcome by righteous indignation.

Judge of the Court of Appeal Otávio took action that very night. He was a tall, agile, vigorous man.

On the following morning he announced to his peers: "Gentlemen, soon you'll see the results of a punitive expedition."

And they all headed for the river.

Around nine o'clock Antonio showed up. From the distance it

could be seen that his upper limbs were tied with blood-drenched rags.

"I cut his arms off at the elbows," the judge of the Court of Appeal explained. "My reliable fish knife hasn't failed me."

Then the grotesque creature drew closer. He was moaning softly.

Just as he had done on the previous day, he entered the river. He tried to thrust his amputated stumps into the water. But the cold made him howl with pain.

Widespread laughter.

Next, the stranger proceeded to intone a monotonous sing-song, his face turned up to the sky. Then he got out of the water and walked past the sportsmen without looking at them.

Later on, people saw the wagon drive away and disappear northward.

Those waters have since not yielded a single fish. There have been no more fishing tournaments at Joy Beach.

WE GUNMEN MUSTN'T FEEL PITY

WE'RE A FEARFUL GUNMAN. WE'RE IN A SALOON IN A SMALL TOWN in Texas. The year is 1880. We're sipping whiskey. There's a doleful expression in our eyes. There are countless deaths in our past. We're filled with remorse. That's why we're drinking.

The door opens. In walks a Chicano named Alonso. He addresses us disrespectfully. He calls us gringo, laughs loudly, makes his spurs clink. We act as if he weren't there. We keep on sipping whiskey. The Chicano walks up to us. He insults us. He gives us a slap on the cheek. Our heart contracts in anguish. We don't feel like killing anyone anymore. But we'll have to make an exception for Alonso, this Chicano dog.

We arrange a duel for the following morning at sunrise. Alonso slaps us on the cheek once more and then leaves. We stand lost in thought, sipping the whiskey. Finally, we toss a gold coin on the counter and leave.

We walk slowly to our hotel. The townsfolk are watching us. They know we are a fearful gunman. Poor Chicano, poor Alonso.

We enter the hotel, climb the stairs to our room, and lie down

27

fully dressed and with our boots on. We lie staring at the ceiling as we smoke. We heave a sigh. We are filled with remorse.

And it is already dawn. We get up. We set our wide belt in place. We submit the gun to the usual inspection. We walk down the stairs.

The street is deserted, but we sense the townsfolk watching us from behind closed curtains. The wind blows, raising small swirls of dust. Ah, this wind! This wind! How many times has it watched us walking slowly, our back turned to the rising sun?

At the end of the street Alonso is already waiting for us. This Chicano really wants to die.

We position ourselves in front of him. He sees a gunman with a doleful expression in his eyes. The grin on his face fades. In our eyes he sees countless deaths. That's what he sees.

We see a Chicano. Poor devil. Soon he won't be eating any more tortillas. His widow and her six kids will bury him at the foot of the hill. They'll lock up their shack and head for Veracruz. The oldest daughter will become a prostitute. The youngest son, a thief.

Our eyes become blurry. Poor Alonso. He shouldn't have slapped us. Now he's terrified. His rotten teeth are chattering. What a pitiful sight.

A tear drops to the dusty ground. It's ours. We place our hand on the holster. But we don't draw the gun. The Chicano does. We see the gun in his hand, we hear the shot, the bullet flies toward our chest, it nestles in our heart. We feel a piercing pain and we slump to the ground.

We die as Alonso, the Chicano, laughs.

We, the gunman, shouldn't have felt pity.

BLIND MAN AND AMIGO GEDEÃO
ALONGSIDE THE HIGHWAY

"THE ONE THAT JUST WENT BY WAS A 1962 VOLKSWAGEN, WASN'T it, amigo Gedeão?"

"No, Blind Man. It was a Simca Typhoon."

"A Simca Typhoon ... ? Ah, yes, that's right. Powerful, the Simca. And very economical. I can tell a Simca Typhoon from a great distance. I can tell any car by the noise of its engine.

"Now this one that just went by was a Ford, wasn't it?"

"No, Blind Man. It was a Mercedes truck."

"A Mercedes truck? You don't say! We haven't had a Mercedes go by in a long time. I can tell a Mercedes from a great distance ... I can tell one car from another. Do you have any idea how long I've been sitting here alongside this highway, listening to all these engines, amigo Gedeão? Twelve years, amigo Gedeão. For twelve years.

"That's an awful long time, amigo Gedeão, wouldn't you say so? Long enough for me to have learned a lot. About cars, I mean. Wasn't this one that just went by a Gordini Willfulness?"

"No, Blind Man. That was a motor scooter."

"A motor scooter ... well, well, they can really deceive a per-

29

son, those motor scooters. 'Specially when the exhaust doesn't
have a muffler.

"But as I was saying, if there's one thing I can do, it's to tell
one car from another by the way the engines sound. Which is
not surprising, really, considering all these years I've spent listening and listening!

"It's an ability that served me well once when ... This one
that just went by was another Mercedes, wasn't it?"

"No, Blind Man. It was a bus."

"That's what I figured. You'd never get two Mercedes in a
row. I said Mercedes just for the heck of it. But where was I?
Ah, yes.

"This ability of mine came in quite handy one time. Would
you care to hear about it, friend Gedeão? Yes? In that case I'll
tell you about it. It'll help while the hours away, right? Thus
the day will end sooner. I like evenings much better: They're
much cooler at this time of the year. But as I was saying, several
years ago a man was killed about two kilometers from here. A
very wealthy farmer, he was. They put fifteen bullets into him.
Wasn't this one that just went by a Galaxy?"

"No. It was a 1964 Volkswagen."

"Ah, a Volkswagen ... Great car. Very economical. The trans-
mission's very good. Well, so they killed this farmer. Haven't you
heard about the case? It was much talked about. Fifteen gunshots.
And they got away with all the money the farmer had on him.
In those days I was already in the habit of sitting here by the
highway and I heard about the crime. It happened on a Sunday.
On Friday I heard it on the radio that the police still didn't have
the slightest clue. Wasn't this one that just went by a Candango."

"No, Blind Man, it wasn't a Candango."

"I was dead sure it was a Candango ... But as I was saying,
it was Friday and they still didn't have a clue.

"I happened to be sitting right here, on this very chair, cud-
geling my brain ... Mulling things over, you know. Until I
reached a conclusion. I decided I should help the police. I asked
my neighbor to tell the district chief of police that I had some
information for them. Sure, this one must have been a Candango."

"No, Blind Man. It was a Gordini Willfulness."

"I could have sworn it was a Candango. The district chief of police wasn't in any big hurry to see me. He probably thought, 'A blind man? What could a blind man have seen?' Or something like that, sheer bunk of course, you know the things they say, amigo Gedeão. Anyway, he ended up coming here because the police were at a loss and willing to interview even a rock. So, the district chief of police, he came here and sat down where you're sitting now, amigo Gedeão. Was this one now the bus?"

"No, Blind Man. That was a pickup, a Chevrolet Peacock."

"A good pickup, too, old but good. Where was I? Ah, yes. The district chief of police came to see me. I asked him: 'What time was it, sir, when the crime was committed?'

"About three in the afternoon, Blind Man.'

"In that case,' I said, 'you should try to locate a 1927 Oldsmobile. The muffler of this car has got a hole in it.

"And there is a defective spark plug. A very fat man was sitting in the front of the car. In the back, I'm sure, there were possibly two or three people.' The district chief of police was flabbergasted. 'How do you know, friend?' was all he kept asking. Wasn't this one that just went by a DKW?"

"No, Blind Man. It was a Volkswagen."

"Yes. The district chief of police was flabbergasted. 'How come you know all this?' 'Well, chief,' I replied, 'it so happens that for years now I've been sitting here next to this highway, listening to the cars go by. I can tell one car from another. And that's not all: I can tell if the engine is in poor shape, if there's too much weight in the front, if there are people on the back seat. It was two-forty-five when this car drove in that direction, and it was three-fifteen when it headed back to the city.' 'How come you knew about the time?' the district chief of police wanted to know. 'Well, Chief,' I replied, 'if there's one thing I can do— aside from being able to tell cars apart by listening to the sound of their engines—it is to tell the time of the day by the position of the sun in the sky.' Although skeptical, the district chief of police went to ... That was an Willys Aero, wasn't it?"

"No, Blind Man. It was a Chevrolet."

"The district chief of police succeeded in locating the 1927 Oldsmobile with the entire gang inside. They were so flabber-

gasted that they gave themselves up without putting up any resistance. The district chief of police recovered all the money
they'd stolen from the farmer, and his family gave me quite a
bundle of a reward. Wasn't the one that went by a Toyota?"

"No, Blind Man. It was a 1956 Ford."

THE PAUSE

AT SEVEN O'CLOCK THE ALARM CLOCK WENT OFF. SAMUEL JUMPED out of bed, dashed into the bathroom, shaved, washed up.

He got dressed quickly and noiselessly. He was in the kitchen making sandwiches when his wife appeared, yawning.

"Going out again, Samuel?"

He nodded in reply. Although young, his hair had already receded from his forehead; but his eyebrows were thick, and even though he had just shaved, his beard had left a bluish shadow on his face. The effect was that of a dark mask.

"You leave so early on Sundays," the woman remarked peevishly.

"There's a backlog of work to get through at the office."

She looked at the sandwiches.

"Why don't you come home for lunch?"

"I've already told you: We have a backlog of work. There's no time. I'm taking something for lunch."

The woman stood scratching her left armpit. Before she had a chance to resume her nagging, Samuel grabbed his hat: "I'll be back this evening."

The streets were still damp with fog. Samuel got the car out

of the garage. He was driving slowly past the waterfront, looking at the idle derricks, at the large barges tied up at the docks.

He parked on a quiet side street. Carrying the bag of sandwiches under his arm, he walked hurriedly for two blocks. He
stopped at the entrance of a small grubby hotel. He glanced
around, then walked in stealthily. He tapped the car keys on
the counter, waking up a small man who sat asleep in an armchair with a torn slipcover. He was the manager. Rubbing his
eyes, he rose to his feet: "Ah, it's you, Senhor Isidoro! You're
earlier than usual today. Nippy outside, isn't it? People—"

"I'm in a hurry, Senhor Raul," Samuel said, cutting him short.

"Okay, I won't keep you." He held out a key. "It's the usual
one."

Samuel climbed four flights up a rickety stairway.

When he reached the top floor, two fat women wearing house-
coats with a floral design looked at him curiously: "Over here,
sweetie!" said one of them. The other laughed.

Gasping for breath, Samuel went into the room and locked
the door behind him. It was a small room: a double bed, a pine
wardrobe; in a corner, a basin filled with water rested on a tri-
pod. Samuel drew the tattered curtains, took a travel alarm clock
out of his pocket, wound it, and placed it on the small bedside
table.

He pulled aside the bedspread and examined the sheets, frown-
ing; sighing, he took off his jacket and his shoes, and loosened
his tie. Seated on the bed, he ate four sandwiches ravenously. He
wiped his fingers on the wrapping paper, lay down, and closed
his eyes.

To sleep.

A moment later, he was asleep. Naked, he was running across
an immense plain, pursued by an Indian on horseback. The gal-
loping echoed in the stuffy room. Over the highlands of the forehead, down the hills of the belly, in the valley between the legs,
they kept running, the pursuer and the quarry.

Samuel tossed about, muttering. At two-thirty in the afternoon he felt a piercing pain in his back. He sat up in bed, his
eyes bulging: The Indian had just pierced him with his spear.
Bleeding to death, soaked with sweat, Samuel sank slowly to

the ground; he heard the gloomy whistle of a steamboat. Then there was silence.

At seven o'clock the alarm clock went off. Samuel jumped out of bed, dashed to the washbasin, and washed up. He got dressed quickly and left.

Seated in the armchair, the hotel manager was reading a magazine.

"Checking out already, Senhor Isidoro?"

"Yeah," said Samuel, handing over the key. He paid and counted his change in silence.

"See you next Sunday, Senhor Isidoro," said the manager.

"Don't know if I'll be back," replied Samuel, looking out the door; night was falling.

"That's what you keep saying, sir, but you always come back," remarked the man, laughing.

Samuel went out.

He drove slowly along the waterfront. He stopped briefly to look at the derricks silhouetted against a reddish sky. Then he drove home.

OF CANNIBALS

In 1950 TWO YOUNG WOMEN WERE FLYING OVER THE DESOLATE tablelands of Bolivia. The plane, a Piper, was being piloted by Barbara, a beautiful woman, tall and blonde, married to a wealthy Mato Grosso rancher. Her companion, Angelina, was slender, dark-complexioned, and had big startled eyes. They were foster sisters.

The sun was sinking below the horizon when the aircraft engine stalled. After some desperate maneuvering, Barbara managed to crash-land on a plateau. The airplane was completely demolished, and the two women found themselves all alone, hundreds of kilometers from the nearest village.

Fortunately (and perhaps having anticipated such a contingency), Barbara had brought a big case containing assorted delicacies: anchovies, Brazil nuts, caviar from the Black Sea, strawberries, broiled kidneys, pineapple compote, soft cheese from Minas, and even bottles of vitamin pills. The case was intact.

The following morning Angelina was hungry, and she asked Barbara for something to eat. Barbara, however, made it very clear that it was impossible for her to comply with Angelina's request, for the food belonged to Barbara, not to Angelina. Resigning herself to this situation, Angelina went off in search of fruits and roots. She found nothing, for the area was completely barren. So she had nothing to eat that day.

Nor did she have anything to eat on the next three days. Barbara, on the other hand, was quite noticeably putting on weight, maybe due to her idleness: She spent the time lying down, eating and waiting for someone to come and rescue them. Angelina kept pacing to and fro, weeping and bemoaning her fate—which merely increased her need for calories.

On the fourth day, while Barbara was eating lunch, Angelina approached her, holding a knife in her hand. Intrigued, Barbara stopped munching—it was a chicken thigh—and stood watching the other woman, who was standing absolutely still. Suddenly, Angelina placed her left hand on a rock, and with a single blow, cut off her ring finger. Blood spouted. Angelina then brought her hand to her mouth and sucked at her own blood.

Since the bleeding wouldn't stop, Barbara made a tourniquet around the stump of her sister's finger. In a few minutes the bleeding stopped. Angelina then took the finger, which had been lying on the ground, wiped it off, and picked the little bones clean. She discarded only the fingernail.

Barbara watched in silence. When Angelina finished eating, Barbara asked her for the bone; then she broke it and used a sliver to pick her teeth. Then the two of them stood talking, reminiscing about childhood events, and so forth and so on.

On the following day Angelina ate the remainder of her fingers, and then her toes. The legs and the thighs followed next.

Barbara helped her prepare the meals, tightened tourniquets whenever necessary, offered advice on how to make the best of the bone marrow, and so forth.

On the fifteenth day, Angelina had to resort to opening up her stomach. The first organ that she removed was the liver. As she was quite hungry, she devoured it raw, although her sister had advised her to fry it first. Consequently, Angelina was still hungry when she finished her meal. She asked Barbara for a piece of bread to soak up the tiny amount of gravy.

Barbara refused her sister's request with the well-reasoned statement she had previously made.

After the spleen and the ovaries, it was the turn of the uterus, which gave Angelina an unpleasant surprise, for she found a large tumor in that organ. Barbara remarked that it must have been the reason why she hadn't been feeling well for months. Angelina agreed, adding, "What a pity I didn't find out about it until now." Then she asked Barbara if it would be harmful to eat the cancer. Barbara advised her to discard that part, which was already showing signs of decay.

On the twentieth day, Angelina passed away; and on the following day a rescue team reached the crash site. On seeing the mangled corpse, they asked Barbara what had happened; and the young woman, bent on preserving her sister's reputation, lied for the first time in her life. "It was the Indians."

The newspapers reported the existence of cannibalistic Indians in Bolivia—which is completely groundless.

THE AGING MARX

BY THE END OF THE LAST CENTURY KARL MARX WAS FEELING rather tired. The political battles were draining him of his energies. His health was poor and he lacked faith in his own future as leader of the international workingmen's movement. He had already accomplished everything he had set out to do. *Das Kapital* had been published and was in circulation; his articles were being studiously read. And yet Marx continued to be ill, poor, and frustrated.

"That's enough," said Marx. "I don't have too many years of life left. I'm going to spend these remaining years incognito, yet comfortably."

It was a painful decision, which brings to mind the story about a man who believed himself to be superior to everybody else because he happened to have six toes on his left foot. He kept mentioning this fact until one day a friend wanted to have a look at those six toes of his. The man then takes off his shoe and sock, and when he looks, he sees that he has five toes, just like everybody else. Widespread laughter. The man goes home,

and feeling somewhat disappointed, he goes to bed. He takes
off his shoe again: There are four toes on his left foot.

Marx was tired out. "I want to enjoy the rest of my life." Marx
made an empirical estimation: He subtracted his age from the
life expectancy for those days and was overcome with anxiety; it
looked as if he didn't have much longer to live. What should
he do? Abandon himself to some playful adventure? But would
it be right to trade austerity for frivolity? To squander in laughter, as the Rosicrucians would say, years of life?

Marx had several daughters. He hoped they would have a better future, a more comfortable life. But how?

Far better than anyone else, Marx understood the foundations
upon which rising capitalism was based. He had aptly diag-
nosed all the errors made by the new industrial society. "I'm in
the best possible position to profit from these very errors," he
thought. Wealth was within his reach.

And yet he hesitated, unable to make a decision. He let the
days slip by, making excuses to his wife: "I've been studying
the best way" ... "I'll have to make some calculations" ... "I
haven't been up to it lately." Irresponsible. Marx was plainly
irresponsible.

His wife and daughters, however, wouldn't be able to bear
their predicament much longer. They had hardly any clothes
to wear. They were down to one meal a day, and that consisted
mostly of potatoes and stale bread.

So, Marx had no other choice but to make up his mind. He
decided to test his theories about easy profits in a new country.
He chose Brazil.

One winter morning at the turn of the century Marx arrived
in Pôrto Alegre. The ship tied up at the fog-shrouded wharf.
Marx and his daughters looked at the barges loaded with or-
anges. The girls, hungry, cried for food. An old gaucho gave
one of them a piece of sausage. The girl devoured it and laughed,
happy.

"Now look at that. A hungry little girl!" said the gaucho,
amazed.

"I'll have to do some research on the role of the proletariat in
underdeveloped countries," Marx was thinking, but soon re-

membered that he was there to make money, not to formulate
theories.

"Let's go!" he said to his family.

They settled at a boarding house located on the old-fashioned
Rua Pantaleão Telles. Soon after their arrival there, another trag-
edy struck the family: The youngest child, Punzi, who had eaten
the sausage, became ill with cramps and diarrhea. Marx, who
couldn't afford to send for a doctor, took her to a public charity
hospital, where she died that same night.

"If you had brought her sooner . . ." said the intern on duty.

In her grief, Marx's wife turned against her husband. "It's your
fault, you damned revolutionary! You're incapable of loving anyone. You know nothing except how to sow hatred everywhere.
You enjoy class warfare, but you're unconcerned about what happens to your own family!"

Feeling contrite, Marx bore with the torrent of abuse.

The following day he went in search of work.

He found a job at a furniture factory on Avenida Cauduro. It
was a small place, dark and dusty; the net income was barely
enough to support the owner, an old bearded Jew. However, the
owner was philosophical about life: "The food that feeds one
person can easily feed two, three, even four people. Especially if
this person is a Jew; even if he happens to be German too."

Besides Marx, two other people worked in the factory: Quirino,
a Negro, and Iossel, a bespectacled youth with a pimply face.
Quirino was skillful at handling the drill, the plane, the gouge,
the chisel, the hammer. He also knew how to use the sanding
machine, and whenever necessary, he worked as the polisher,
too. There was nobody who could handle the band saw as well
as he.

Iossel would lend them a hand occasionally. He spoke to Marx
one day: "Would you like to join us? I belong to a group of
good Jewish youths. We take turns meeting at one another's houses
and discuss a variety of subjects. We intend to marry good girls
and have families of our own. We want to improve the quality
of life in our community. Would you like to participate in our
meetings, Karl Marx?"

Marx declined the invitation for two reasons: First, after hav-

ing written "On the Jewish Question," he believed he had nothing new to say about the Jewish people; second, his goal was to
make money, not to fraternize.

"I can't join you, Iossel. My objective is to succeed in life. I
advise you to put illusions aside. Turn your energies to something serious before it's too late. Your health is already suffering.
You'll end up dying of tuberculosis."

Indeed, although tuberculosis is rare among the Jews, Iossel
began to cough up blood and he died without having started a
family of his own. The old man, Marx, and the Negro Quirino
attended the burial. Some young men with frightened expressions on their faces showed up at the cemetery. Marx supposed
that they were members of the discussion group. He was right:
Marx was hardly ever wrong nowadays.

Before going to bed one night, Marx looked at his left foot.
"Five toes!" he said aloud. "Four previously; six someday!"

"What?" asked his wife sleepily.

"Go back to sleep, woman," he replied.

Marx followed the economic predicament carefully. He read
everything he could lay his hands on: newspapers, magazines,
books. He listened to the radio; to what people were talking about
on the street corners. He gathered data. He examined trends.

The factory owner was getting on in years. One day he called
Marx into his office: "I'm an old man. I need a partner. How
would you like to become my partner?"

"But I have nothing."

"That's all right. I trust your Jewish integrity, even though
you're a German too."

Marx accepted the offer. There were two of them now to boss
the Negro Quirino about. Quirino didn't mind, though: He
would rush from the sanding machine to the band saw, from
the band saw to the wood polisher, and in between, he would
nail down a slat, always crooning "My Precious Darling."

Slowly at first, but like an engine gradually picking up speed,
Marx worked. Before his arrival, the factory operated on a simple system: A customer would come to the factory, order, say, a
wardrobe—giving his own specifications for size and shape—
and even stipulate the price.

After the contract was sealed with a handshake, everybody—
boss and employees—set to work. Marx put an end to this disor-
ganized way of doing things. He announced that an assembly
line would be instituted. But first he fired the Negro Quirino.

"But why?" protested the old man. "Such a good employee!
He can do everything."

"Precisely for that reason," replied Marx. "I want people who
are capable of doing just one thing: specialists, do you follow
me? People who are able to handle the gouge, the plane, the band
saw equally well, people who are skillful at everything—well, I
have no use for them!"

"But you don't know a thing about furniture!" The old man
was desolate.

"But I *do* know about economics. Why don't you go to bed,
partner?"

World War II was just beginning. Marx, who had already shaved
off his beard, raised the Brazilian flag at the factory. He spoke
perfect Portuguese; nobody would have guessed that he was a
European. However, he was smart enough to take precautions.
He had just entered into a contract with the army to manufacture furniture and he didn't want his foreign status to jeopar-
dize his business.

The old man spent his days at the synagogue.

There was horrifying news from Europe. Concentration camps.
Gas chambers . . . One day while they were sitting drinking
coffee, Marx's wife said: "You were right about saying that there's
a line of blood running across the history of mankind," and
she helped herself to some butter.

Churchill was offering blood, sweat, and tears to the English-
men. Marx had a loudspeaker system installed at the factory in
order to broadcast patriotic anthems as well as requests for increased productivity on the part of the workers. "London has
been suffering bombings! And what about you, what have you
been doing?" He was one of the very first entrepreneurs to in-
vest in an advertising campaign. Thanks to his vision and other
qualities, he made a lot of money.

True, there was no continuity or smoothness in his method.
The floods of 1941 were a major setback. Thousands of hard-

wood planks floated away in the muddy waters: Marx accepted
this blow with resignation. "Man has turned himself into a giant
by controlling the forces of nature," he thought.

On the other hand, at the time of the floods, the old man came
down with pneumonia and died. Marx was relieved: He just
couldn't stand his partner's admonitions anymore. However, Marx
had the old man's portrait hung in the office and he made a
touching speech on the occasion.

He was still to suffer through a major moral crisis. It happened toward the end of the war: The Russian troops were
marching across Europe, leaving tumult in their wake. Red flags
were being raised in various capitals.

"Could I have been right after all?" Marx wondered, alarmed.
"Will the proletariat gain power after all? Will the capitalists
be crushed? Will the guts of the last landowner be used to hang
the last financier?"

He decided to put his old theories to the test. If they proved
to be wrong, he would acknowledge his mistake and help the
proletariat win the class war.

In one of his factories, there was an apprentice named Quirininho.
He was the Negro Quirino's son. Marx decided to use him as a
guinea pig.

Marx called him.

"Quirininho."

"Yes, sir?"

"Clean my shoes."

Smiling, Quirininho cleaned Marx's shoes.

"Quirininho."

"Yes, sir?"

"You're an idiot."

"Yes, sir."

"Don't you realize that everything here belongs to you? These
machines are yours, the furniture that you've made is yours,
the mansion where I live is yours. You could become the lover
of one of my daughters if you wanted to. The future belongs
to you."

"Yes, sir."

"Don't you want to own this factory?"

"You're pulling my leg, Senhor Marx!" the Brazilian-born Negro said, grinning widely.

"I'm not pulling your leg, you idiot!" Marx was shouting at him. "Take over this factory! It belongs to you. Go on strike! Set up barricades!"

Quirininho remained silent, staring at the floor.

"What is it that you want most in life?"

"To own a small house in Vila Jardim. To go to a soccer game every Sunday. To drink rum with my friends on Saturday nights. To get married. To be happy."

Every night Marx counted his toes.

"Are there six now?" his wife would ask, mocking him.

She, too, died. Marx set up a special fund in her memory.

Now that he was getting on in years, Marx became embittered. One of his daughters got married to the owner of an airline company. He didn't go to the wedding. Another daughter eloped with the company's accountant. He didn't care.

What was Marx's secret? He was always riding the crest of the wave. He noticed trends. "There's bound to be a housing shortage, what with all these people emigrating from the rural areas in search of the attractions of the big cities." And he rushed headlong into investing in real estate. He made use of psychology: He offered things like Security, with a capital S. He made friends with everyone in the financial world; lines of credit were always open to him. In times of recession, he offered financing at high interest rates.

Now that he was getting on in years, Marx became embittered. He drank unsweetened maté, which he had always abhorred. Gloomily sucking up the bitter liquid through a straw, he grumbled about the modern entrepreneurs. ("Bums. Bums and idiots. Don't know a thing about economics. Can't function at all without a computer. They lack vision. I've always been able to predict a crisis with the precision of a stopwatch without ever having to resort to a computer.") He grumbled about the communist countries. ("They quarrel among themselves like a bunch of gossips. And all they can think of is expenditure.") He complained about the maté. ("It's cold, stone cold!")

Quirininho was mortally injured in an accident at the factory.

Before he died he wanted to see his boss, whom he asked humbly for his blessing.

Marx was deeply impressed. Three days later Marx was hospitalized and his left foot had to be amputated. He insisted on having it embalmed and buried, with a solemn funeral ceremony. Representatives from the upper echelons were present at the burial; ill at ease, they exchanged glances.

Marx died many years ago.

During some antileftist demonstrations, the foot was exhumed by an infuriated crowd. Before they burned it, someone observed that it had six toes.

LEO

LEO, THE JEWISH BOY: IN THE LIQUID BROWN EYES, THE REMAINS
of small villages in Poland. The smile, rare and sorrowful.

Leo's father was a tall, strong cabinetmaker who worked hard
and didn't make much money. At times he suffered from head-
aches and would moan softly. Leo's mother cooked the meals and
intoned sad songs in Yiddish. On Fridays she sacrificed a fish
from the sea. The family sat around the table covered with a
white tablecloth. By the light of the candles, they apportioned
the food. The father was given the head; he ate it slowly. Then
he sucked at the bones of the flattened skull.

They lived in a frame house located on a side street. At the
far end of the big backyard there was a wooden shed, kept
padlocked, and inside which Leo had never been.

It was winter . . . Every morning, dark-complexioned boys took
their fishing rods and went fishing in the river.

Leo stood at the window, watching the street. He couldn't go
fishing. He looked after the house while his father worked at
the furniture factory and his mother shopped at the open-air market. Leo couldn't go out.

Once it rained for days on end. One morning Leo went to the kitchen door and looked out: The backyard was flooded. He got dressed, said good-bye to his mother and started to row. He hoisted his flag up the mast and sounded the vastness of the waters.

The boat sailed the waters dauntlessly. The nights went by, star-studded. From the crow's nest, Leo watched and thought of all the magnificent adventurers: John, The Englishman, who had climbed the Himalayas with one of his hands tied behind his back; Fred, who had set off on a journey inside a barrel launched in the Gulf of Mexico and had been picked up off Pintada Island a year later; Boris, the blood brother of a Comanche chief.

Leo lived on fish and algae; he wrote entries in his logbook and gazed at the islands. The natives watched him sail by—a morose man, keeping himself aloof from the waters, aloof from the skies. Once there was a storm. But it didn't defeat him, it didn't!

And what about the monsters? What is there to say about them since nobody has ever seen them?

"Leo, come in and have lunch!" his mother shouted.

Leo was sailing afar; off the coast of Africa.

One day he came back. From then on, he was never again free.

A winter afternoon. The pale sun was sliding across the sky. At the furniture factory, his father worked with the sanding machine, his head white with dust. He stacked up cupboard doors amid heaps of sawdust. The boss would come and yell at him in Yiddish.

His mother baked a fish for the approaching night, the holy Sabbath night. She was pregnant and moved about with diffi- culty. In the cold, rarefied air, pigeons fluttered about sluggishly, looking furtive. At the far end of the backyard, there was the padlocked shed.

They ate dinner in silence. His parents went to bed. In the kitchen sink, a stack of dishes, still with the remains of fish. The cupboard doors made snapping sounds.

Leo couldn't sleep; he was running a temperature. He was

crying softly, his damp hands holding his treasure: a fishing
line and a fishhook. Everything was enveloped in darkness. In
this darkness Leo got up and began to walk. He walked across
the narrow hall, across the kitchen, toward the backyard. It was
past eleven o'clock, it was past midnight.

Leo stepped out into the chilly night. He walked, at first leaning against the slimy wall, then without propping himself up.
Left behind were the house, his father and his mother.

He reached the shed. He bent down, inserted the fishing line
and the fishhook under the big door, and stood waiting. Motionless beneath the sky, confined by the wall, Leo stood waiting. Inside him, something was growing and throbbing.

He stood waiting. Suddenly, he felt the fishing line quiver. A
signal? He didn't dare pull it. He was afraid. He wanted to let
go and flee. But he controlled himself; he waited; and there he
stood, peaceful and very quiet, ready for the long vigil. And when
the fishing line quivered again, he pulled it with all his strength.

Something jumped up into the air and fell into his arms.

It was a fish; a pitiful animal, a wretched creature of the water. Surely it must have lived in the deepest depths, for it was
eyeless. Leo had plucked it from the depths and now he was holding it in his lap. He examined the fish, its bruised skin, its grotesque fins. He examined its twisted mouth, which at times
emitted a faint moan. Leo stroked its absurd head.

He was crying softly; he was running a temperature. In Poland, the villages lay asleep.

A HOUSE

A CERTAIN MAN STILL DIDN'T HAVE A HOUSE OF HIS OWN WHEN he suffered a heart attack. The pain was quite severe and as usual under such circumstances, he felt close to death. He asked the doctor who examined him how much longer he would live.

"Who knows?" replied the doctor. "Maybe one day, maybe ten years."

The man was deeply impressed, something he hadn't experienced in a long time. He led a peaceful life. He was retired. Every day he got up, read the newspaper (limiting himself to the entertainment and leisure sections), walked as far as Alfândega Square, talked to his friends there, had his shoes shined. Then he would have lunch, take a nap, and listen to the radio in the afternoons. In the evenings he watched television. All these things lulled his soul soothingly, without making any great demands on him. Since he was single and his parents were dead, he was free from care; he lived in a room in a boarding house, and his landlady—a kindly woman—looked after everything.

But then the man sees his life draining away. While washing up, he watches the water in the washbasin flowing down the

53

drain. "That's how it is." He wipes his face dry; he combs his hair carefully. "At least a home." Any kind: A cottage, a tiny apartment, even a basement would do. But to die in his own house. At home.

He looks for a real estate agency. The real estate agent shows him house designs and photographs. The man looks at them, perplexed. He's unable to choose. He doesn't know if he needs two bedrooms or three. There's one house with air-conditioning, but will he live until the summer?

Suddenly, he finds it: "This one. I'll buy it." The photograph shows an old wooden bungalow, with colonial-style eaves and faded paintwork. "This one is on the market just for the lot," explains the real estate agent. "The house itself is falling apart." "It doesn't matter." The real estate agent tries to reason with him: "It's quite far away ..." Far away! The man smiles. He signs the papers, gets the keys, jots down the address, and leaves.

The day is drawing in and the man moves among people in the streets, feeling elated. He is about to move into his own house! In a square near his boarding house some draymen stand waiting for a customer. The man talks to one of them and hires his services.

It takes the drayman just a few minutes to place the baggage on his cart, but it's dark night when they start out. The man is silent throughout the trip. He hasn't said good-bye to his land-lady. After giving the address to the drayman, he hasn't ut-tered a single word.

The cart moves slowly along the deserted streets. Lulled by the movement, the man dozes off—and he has dreams, visions or recollections: old songs; his mother calling him in at coffee time; the sound of the school bell.

"Here we are," says the drayman. The man opens his eyes: It's the same house he saw in the photograph. Impulsively, the man grabs the drayman's hand, thanking him and wishing all the best. The man feels like inviting the other in: "Come in and have tea with me." But there is no tea. The drayman takes his money and leaves, coughing.

The man carries his belongings indoors, shuts the door and double-locks it. He lights a candle. He looks about: at the floor strewn with dead insects and shreds of paper, at the dirty walls. He feels very tired. He spreads a blanket on the floor and lies down, wrapping his overcoat around him.

The floorboards creak and he can hear whispers; the voices sound familiar: Father, Mother, Aunt Rafaela; they are all here— even Grandfather, with his ironic feigned laughter.

No, the man is not afraid. His heart—a piece of dried-out leather, as he imagines it to be—keeps beating in the usual rhythm. He falls asleep, life goes out, and it is already morning.

It's morning; but the sun hasn't risen. The man gets up and opens the window; a cold gray light seeps into the room. It's neither sunlight nor moonlight. And by this light he sees the street that runs along in front of the house. A fragment of street, emerging from the fog and ending in it. There are no other houses; or, if there are, he can't see them. The bungalow looks out on an empty lot where, half-covered by vegetation, lies the rusty skeleton of an old Packard.

An animal jumps out of the empty lot into the road. It's an outlandish creature: It looks like a rat but is almost as big as a donkey. "What kind of animal could it be?" wonders the man. In high school he used to like zoology quite a lot; he had studied the ornithorhynchus and the zebra in detail; and the rodent as well. He had wanted to become a zoologist, but friends showing good judgment had dissuaded him from pursuing a career which, according to them, didn't exist—unless proven otherwise. Nevertheless, seeing this strange specimen has jolted him. And the man has barely recovered from this jolt when he hears someone whistling.

Out of the mists steps a man. A short, dark-complexioned man who looks like an Indian. He walks slowly, tapping on the stones with a shepherd's staff; and he keeps on whistling.

"Good morning!"

The aborigine doesn't reply. He stops walking, then stands smiling and staring.

Somewhat perplexed, the man persists: "Do you live around here?"

Still smiling, the wanderer murmurs a few words in some exotic language and disappears.

"It's an exotic language," the man thinks. So, he must be in some distant country. The real estate agent had certainly warned him. But that was a long time ago.

Disoriented, the man decides to go to the top floor, from where he hopes to find his bearings. He runs toward the stairway, climbs up the steps two at a time ("and there's no sign of angina!"), reaches what looks like a turret, and opens its tiny windows. The fog has lifted and he is able to see. And what does he see?

Rivers scintillating along prairies, that's what he sees; lakes abounding in fish, huge forests, snow-covered peaks, volcanoes. He spots the sea in the distance; and in the harbors, caravels lie at anchor. He can even see sailors climbing the mast and letting down the canvas.

"Yes, it's another country," the man concludes. "And I'll have to start from scratch."

It could be about ten in the morning—that is, if hours still counted—and the temperature might be said to be pleasant.

The man starts off by removing his overcoat.

THE PHANTOM TRAIN

FINALLY, IT WAS CONFIRMED: MATIAS'S DISEASE WAS INDEED LEU-
kemia, and his mother sent for me. In tears, she told me that
Matias's greatest wish had always been to take a ride on the
Phantom Train; she would like to grant him this wish now, and
she counted on me. Matias was nine years old. I was ten. I
scratched my head.

It would be impossible to take him to the park where the Phantom Train was. We would have to improvise something in his
house, an old mansion in Moinhos Velhos, full of dark furniture
and wine-colored velvet curtains. Matias's mother gave me some
money; I went to the park and took a ride on the Phantom Train.
I did so several times. And wrote everything down on a sheet
of paper, just as I'm doing now. I also drew a diagram. Having
this data on hand, we set up our own Phantom Train.

The event took place at 9:00 P.M. on July 3, 1956. The cold
winter wind from the southwest was hissing through the trees,
but the house was quiet. We woke up Matias. He was shivering
with cold; his mother wrapped him in blankets. Taking the utmost care, we placed him in a baby carriage. He was so withered

now that he fit inside. I took him to the entrance hall of the old mansion and there we stood waiting on the marble floor.

The lights went out. It was the signal. Pushing the baby carriage, I dashed headlong, running at full speed down the long hall. The drawing room door opened; I went in. There stood Matias's mother, dressed up like a witch (her face plastered with red makeup; her painted eyes, wide open; black apparel; on her shoulder, a stuffed owl; she was invoking evil spirits).

I went around the drawing room twice, always pursued by the woman. Matias shrieked with fright and pleasure. I returned to the hall.

Another door opened—into the bathroom; an old-fashioned bathroom full of potted ferns and faucets of burnished bronze. Dangling from the shower head was Matias's father: a hanged man, his tongue protruding, his face a purplish blue.

After leaving the bathroom, I entered a bedroom where Matias's brother was lying—he was a skeleton (on his thin thorax, the ribs had been painted with phosphorescent paint; in his hands, a rusty chain).

In the den we found Matias's two sisters, who'd been stabbed (the knives buried in their breasts; their faces smeared with chicken blood; from one of them, the sound of the death rattle).

That was what the Phantom Train was like in 1956.

Matias was exhausted. His brother lifted him out of the baby carriage and, with the utmost care, laid him on his bed.

His parents were crying softly. His mother wanted to give me some money. I didn't take it. I ran home.

Matias died a few weeks later. To the best of my recollection, I have never taken a ride on the Phantom Train since then.

THE DAY WHEN WE KILLED JAMES CAGNEY

ONE DAY WE WENT TO THE APOLLO MOVIE THEATER.

Since it was a Sunday matinee, we expected to see a good movie, with the hero being the winner. We ate coffee candy and kept hitting each other on the head with our comic books. When the lights were turned off, we cheered and whistled, but soon after the opening scenes, we began to have some misgivings ...

The hero, whose name was James Cagney, was quite short and he didn't hit anybody. Quite the opposite: Every time he ran into the bad guy—a tall fellow called Sam—this guy, who sported a large mustache, would beat the living daylights out of him. There were punches and blows and a monkey wrench, and even kicks aimed at his belly. James Cagney was beaten to a pulp—he was a bloody mess, with a swollen eye—and he didn't fight back.

At first we just grumbled, but soon we were stomping our feet. It was impossible for us to respect or hold in high regard such a despicable milksop.

James Cagney had led a wretched life. He had to earn a living when he was still quite young. He used to sell newspapers on the street corner. Street kids were always trying to steal money from him, but he had always defended himself bravely. And now look at what had become of his promising career! Yes, we booed him and called him all kinds of names.

James Cagney began to show signs that he was afraid of us. He would slip away, flattening himself against walls. He looked at us sideways. Dastardly dog, scoundrel, traitor!

Three months later into the movie, Sam gives him another whopping thrashing and he is left sprawled on the floor, bleeding like a pig. We had just about given up on him. Quite frankly, we felt so disgusted with him that, as far as we were concerned, he could just die there once and for all—such was the degree of our revulsion.

But then one of us noticed a faint twitching in the fingers of his left hand and a discreet tightening of his lips.

In a man lying beaten up on the ground, such signs could be considered encouraging.

We decided that in spite of everything, it would be worthwhile to root for James Cagney. We began to cheer, moderately but resolutely.

James Cagney rose to his feet. We clapped our hands somewhat more loudly—not too clamorously, however, just enough to keep him on his feet. We made him walk a few steps. When he comes to a mirror, he should take a good look at himself, that's what we are hoping for at that moment.

James Cagney looked at himself in the mirror. We stood in silence as he watched his shame surfacing on his battered face.

"Get your revenge on him!" somebody shouted. It was quite unnecessary, though: To the wise, our silence was sufficient, and James Cagney had already learned enough from us that Sunday afternoon there in the Apollo movie theater.

Slowly he began to pull open a drawer in the dresser, and then he took out his father's old gun. He examined it: It was a .45 revolver. We were now whistling and clapping our hands wildly. James Cagney put on his hat and made a dash for his car. His hands gripped the steering wheel firmly; his face showed determination. We had made a new man of James Cagney. We let him know that we approved of the self-confident expression in his eyes.

He found Sam in a third-rate hotel. He climbed the stairs slowly. We punctuated his footsteps by rhythmically stamping our lace-up boots on the floor. When he opened the bedroom door, we broke into some deafening screaming.

Sam was sitting on the bed. He rose to his feet. He was a giant of a man. James Cagney looked at the bad guy, then he looked at us. We had to admit it: He was afraid. All our hard work, all our efforts during all those weeks proved to be in vain. James Cagney continued to be James Cagney. The bad guy grabbed the .45 away from him and shot him right in the middle of his forehead: He fell to the ground without a moan.

"It serves him right," muttered Pedro, when the lights were turned on. "He richly deserved it."

It was our first crime. We have committed many others since then.

VEGETABLE KINGDOM

IN THE VEGETABLE KINGDOM. THAT'S WHAT GLORIA SAYS: WE
live in the vegetable kingdom, amid giant ferns, maidenhair, rubber trees, boa constrictors, green tumid growing things unfold-
ing their leaves throughout the house. It's Marina who looks
after them, as well as after everything else. Marina cooks, Gloria
spruces herself up. Marina sews, Gloria makes bantering re-
marks. Gloria sleeps, Marina keeps vigil. Marina does needle-
work and cleans and polishes. She makes buttonholes and covers
for the buttons; she embroiders and she knits. Proficient in the
domestic arts, people say about her. She makes and sells artifi-
cial flowers. The income that she gets from this work makes up
a substantial amount of her domestic budget and even provides
her with enough reserve funds for a rainy day. Hardworking as
an ant, that's what Marina is like. As for Gloria, she sings before the mirror, makes up her face, examines the skin on her
face anxiously. But after all—wonder the neighbors—which
one is the mother, which one is the daughter?

Gloria is the mother. She was born earlier. She got married,
conceived Marina and became a widow. She mourned the death

63

of her husband, but not overly so; then she forgot him. She's got
her daughter, who brightens her days, but only with a dim light.
However, the light is bright enough to chase away the shadows
that rise from the dead corners of the house and from amid
the ferns.

Marina looks after her mother and their house, moving about
silently in the kitchen. After lunch, while Gloria lies snoring,
she sits down by the stove, lights a cigarette and with a scowl (she
cultivates wrinkles, says Gloria) stares at the cracks in the walls.

And it's three in the afternoon. Soon a sunbeam ("the witch's
little horse," says Marina) will seep into the bedroom through
a slit in the venetian blind. Marina will sit down on the bed,
place Gloria's head in her lap, and wake her gently. "Mummy,
mummy," Gloria, still half-asleep, will murmur. "Can I have some
chocolate?" "Yes, my little daughter," Marina will say, kissing
her rosy cheeks. She'll help Gloria get dressed; she'll let her go
for a walk in the main square, but she'll ask her to be home
by five, when a strong breeze starts to blow in the square.

Alone in the empty house, Marina will think a little about
her own childhood, about the doll with the blond hair. She'll com-
press her lips, pushing these memories aside with a small gesture, and she'll water the boa constrictor, which grows luxuriantly,
displaying a mass of strong sinews, before her admiring eyes.
There was a time when Marina was afraid that this plant might
be carnivorous, then a time when she laughed at such fears,
but now she neither fears nor laughs: She merely tightens her
lips and proceeds to get dinner ready.

Gloria returns, her face aglow, and announces that she has a
secret to tell.

"Do tell me," says Marina, her eyes blank. But now Gloria
doesn't want to: "After dinner ..." Marina serves her soup;
she places a napkin around Gloria's neck so that she won't soil
her new blouse. "Tell me now," she insists. Gloria laughs, claps
her hands: She's being naughty; she won't tell. And on top of
that, she slurps her soup, knowing that Marina can't stand it.
Marina doesn't like noises.

After dinner they'll sit on the sofa. Marina will light a cigarette, Gloria will rest her head on Marina's shoulder and will

talk about the man who keeps following her in the square. "He's tall, with a dark complexion. His face is grave ..." She would like to become his girlfriend. "Will you let me?"

Marina will hesitate; and she won't have to reply because by then Gloria will already be dozing off. A moonbeam—the witch's little mule—slides over the wooden floor of the living room. The vine begins to unfurl its long, thin stems. A thousand eyes glitter from amid the leaves of the ferns. They are drops of water, Marina believes.

NAVIGATION CHART

The time: 7:30. Distance from the island: about 800 meters. Distance from the bank of the river: zero (note—boat run aground). Depth of the water: 20 centimeters at most. Facial expression: normal (big brown eyes, wide open; mouth, half-open). Normal.

THE ISLAND WAS THERE, EIGHT HUNDRED METERS FROM THE bank: We didn't dare reach it by swimming. We were small boys; besides, our parents had warned us about the dangers of the Guaíba—a treacherous river, full of currents.

But the island was there, a small stretch of land covered with thick, wild vegetation. During the floods only the top leafage of the trees stood visible, and there the corpses of animals floating down the river got entangled. Caught in the branches, the carcasses would slowly decay, and then when the waters receded, the skeletons were left bleaching in the branches.

Nowadays we know this. However, in those days, when we looked through the binoculars (whose binoculars were they?) and saw the bulls' skulls on the treetops, we wanted to find out who had placed them there. Indians?

Then we discovered the boat. An old canoe run aground amid the sedge. It was filled with greenish water; as we came closer, a small snake slithered away from it and disappeared into the vegetation.

That greenish water—it would delight Rogério nowadays; he is a biologist. Ah, the things he would notice today in that water. Paramecia, amoebas, tiny worms, various larvae—all of them living in a stagnant world, but a stagnant world seething with creatures moving about frantically in search of things, of food—and in their search constantly colliding with one another. Today Rogério knows. We turned the boat over and drained out the putrid water, which then vanished into the hot, coarse sand, leaving tiny creatures flitting about in the air; later, they grew quiet. Egg shells. A pack of Continental cigarettes. Assorted bits and pieces.

The boat returned to its normal position and it was ready to sail.

Then we turned to him and said: Climb in.

The time: 8:05. Distance to the island: the same. Distance from the bank: the same. Depth of the water: the same. Facial expression: surprise; mild apprehension, noticeable only in a slight frown.

Yes, you, we insisted.

He was the youngest and the lightest among us.

But those weren't the only reasons. There were others: He could be silent when it was time to be silent; when he was supposed to look, he looked, and when he was supposed to listen, he listened, his mouth half open, his big brown eyes wide open ... And when he was supposed to speak, he spoke; he'd tell us everything; his dreams, other people's dreams, his brothers' ...

But where in the world does he hear—we wondered, intrigued—all these things? (*Lies,* all these *lies,* we were about to say, but didn't, for after all how could we know for sure whether they were lies? What if they were indeed the truth?)

Now he was refusing to go. I'm afraid, he said; and we prodded him on. Come on, don't be such a drag; you're dying to go. For how could we know whether he was telling us the truth?

Wasn't it possible that he was just whining? (This happened in the early fifties, when there were plenty of coy people around; plenty of people who jawed away; plenty of drivelers.) Cut it out and climb in, we told him.

And we began to push him—but not roughly, because then he would just go to pieces. We jostled him gently, playfully, even tenderly; he kept resisting, but without much conviction, without the inflexibility of someone refusing to budge another inch, or of someone who would rather die than give in. Maybe he was simply unable to offer any resistance, for he was rather frail. Anyway, when he found himself hemmed in by the boat behind him and by us closing in on him—with our laughter, our hands, our fingernails, our eyes, our freckles, our hair—it was with an almost automatic gesture that he raised a leg over the side of the boat. Then he realized that he was halfway in it, and he still could have taken his leg out again—but did he want to, did he? Anyway, he didn't take his leg out; he hesitated for a while, then moved the other leg inside the boat. Was it an automatic gesture? Was it an inner voice that commanded him to do so? Was it a conscious decision, a prudent act of submission?

Then we looked, and he looked, and all of us realized that he was in the boat.

The time: 8:35. Distance to the island: the same. Distance from the bank: the same. Depth of the water: the same. Facial expression: changeable according to each individual onlooker: artful conniv- ance (Rui, nowadays a merchant); calm despair (Alberto, nowadays a priest); sheer terror (Jorge, nowadays a journalist).

From then on he did whatever we told him to do. Sit down in the boat, we said, and he sat down. Take the paddle and he took the paddle, which was a board taken from a packing case.

When you reach the island, we told him, beach the boat, tie it securely, get off the boat, walk around, go into the bushes and look around very carefully; but if there are any Indians, hide yourself; steal a skull . . .

Frozen still, he sat listening to us in silence.

He was staring at us; we stared back. We kept consulting

among ourselves, exchanging glances: What if there's a house there, should he go in? Should he speak to anyone he finds there?

And we began to push the boat into the water, into the river.

Push! we shouted at each other. Push! The boat was heavy. Push! We managed to move it a few centimeters, then a few more—

Then we realized that it was floating away.

Start rowing! we shouted. Row!

But he didn't row. He sat staring at us.

The time: 8:40. Distance to the island: about 750 meters. Distance from the bank: 50 meters (note—boat moving). Depth of the water: 4 to 5 meters. Facial expression: (nobody noticed).

Start rowing! Come on, row! we shouted anxiously.

The time: 8:55. Distance to the island: about 600 meters. Distance from the bank: 200 meters (note: boat moving rapidly). Depth of the water: 20 to 30 meters. Facial expression: impossible to describe; kept facing the island.

This fog, the fog that enveloped everything at that moment isn't—wasn't—unusual . . . No, it isn't. For a couple of hours it was impossible to see a thing. We shouted, but got no reply.

When the fog lifted, there was no sign of the boat. The island was there, and so were the trees and the skulls, but the boat wasn't.

And we didn't even know where he lived. We didn't even know his full name.

The time: 10:15. Distance to the island: about 500 meters. Distance from the bank: 300 meters. Depth of the water: 20 to 30 meters. Facial expressions (ours): peaceful, generally speaking.

We come here sometimes. The entire old gang, now aboard Rui's boat (almost as big as a yacht).

We don't talk about the island, but we glance at it.

There's now a bridge connecting it to the bank—to *the other bank*, not ours. The trees are still there but the bulls' skulls are gone. And there's some construction work going on there—a factory, it seems. The concrete uprights loom off-white against the dark green of the vegetation. And there are smokestacks.

Who owns it? I ask, but get no reply. The time is 10:30, the distance from the island is four hundred meters, and the facial expressions—of the ones I can see—show calm indifference.

ECOLOGY

THERE WAS A TIME WHEN THIS ENTIRE AREA WAS QUITE PASTO-
ral, you know. The meadow, the birds, the breeze, the brook.
Very peaceful, it used to be around here.

No so anymore. Now, things happen. For example, the two
dots that have just appeared on the horizon. They advance
slowly; finally, they take form. It's a couple. He, a fat, elderly
man wearing a white suit, a red tie, and a Panama hat; he wipes
his sweaty face with a large handkerchief. (I recognize the linen
in the white suit: the fibers from the plants that used to grow
in a meadow similar to this one. Poor fibers; poor plants.)

The woman is also fat and dumpy. She is sweaty, too, but she
doesn't wipe her face; she keeps muttering. (I recognize the silk
in the woman's dress: a substance extracted from a larva's co-
coon, and then made into thread, and then dyed, and then cut
up, and then sewn. Poor larvae; poor substance.)

They are approaching. They come nearer. Now they are three
meters away, at most. They raise their eyes, then hug each other
and burst into tears. That's right: They're crying. And they cry
and cry . . . Finally, the man wipes his tears with the handker-

73

chief. (I recognize the cotton in it. Poor cotton.) He takes a step forward, keeping his eyes raised all the time, and says in a tearful voice: "Come down, daughter. Come down and speak to your parents." He cuts a sorry figure, this tearful old man. "We had a hard time finding you, my daughter. We took a plane, then a bus ... And we had to cover this final stretch of country on foot because there are no roads here ... Ah, my daughter, we're dead tired, daughter. Come down and talk to us."

Silence.

A lie: There's never absolute silence here because of the breeze, of the birds; but they are nature's sounds. Whereas these sobs, this puffing and panting ... No. They are not nature's. They are something revolting.

"Come down, my daughter." The old man has resumed his litany. "Did you ever see anyone living in a treetop like that? What are you, an animal? No, of course you're not an animal, my daughter. Come down now, come down and embrace your parents. Come down, will you? We'll forgive you everything."

There's no reply.

"Don't you realize you're killing your mother?"

Ah, this sounds like an outrage. The effrontery!

"Come down, my daughter. Come down, for God's sake!"

Now it is the old woman's turn to shout in her shrill voice. "Take a good look at your face! Just look at your hair. It looks like chaff."

Chaff. Yeah, I know. It's what remains of the wheat, of the hay, after they thresh them, after they ... But I'd rather not talk about it. The brutes. Poor plants, poor chaff.

"Daughter, listen!" (It's the old woman again.) "I've brought you some apples, my daughter. Come down, and eat with us, daughter. Apples, look! You like them so much."

Apples! Now, that's the limit. So they dared pluck apples from a tree. And now they have the gall to offer them to me. But what kind of people are they? The two of them would be perfectly capable of roasting a child and then offer him to his mother.

"Come down, daughter!"

Never.

"Come down!"

Let them shout to their hearts' content.

Time goes by. We know for a fact that time does go by here. We have, as we know, the days and the nights, the rain and the sunshine, the heat, the cold, the heat. Right now, for example, night is falling. There's logic and certainty in this fact. But they, the old couple, don't know that night falls here. They are startled, look around them, and exchange words in a low voice. What are they afraid of? Animals? Poor animals!

They make a hasty departure. The old man turns around once: "We'll be back tomorrow, my daughter."

Let them come back. It's no concern of mine. You know: *I am the tree.*

BEFORE MAKING THE INVESTMENT

WE DIDN'T HAVE MONEY FOR A BUS TICKET TO THE NEXT CITY, therefore my friend suggested that we board a freight train—the transportation system used by shrewd people. As soon as night began to fall, we made a dash for one of the empty boxcars, where he hid ourselves. Panting, we slid the heavy door shut and then lay down on the floor. We were tired and hungry.

Then I smelled something.

"Amigo, do you detect something strange in here?"

He didn't reply. I ignored the smell. Then I noticed that we were lying on a thin layer of straw. Much too thin, as a matter of fact—yet we seemed quite far away from the real floor of the boxcar.

"Not much straw in here, is there?"

In the dark, I could hear him panting. He heaved a sigh and said: "Amigo, you ask too many questions. Why don't you shut up and try to get some sleep? We have a lot to do tomorrow."

My friend dislikes unnecessary questions. I, however, have an inborn curiosity. My father used to say that I would be a scientist. God has already forgiven him his mistake and he rests in peace.

I kept thinking and asking myself questions while my fingers explored the straw. However, I didn't want my friend to notice that I was carrying on my investigation; he could take offense at what I was doing. I asked him casually: "Amigo, what's the name of this city?"

"You know it, amigo," he muttered.

"Yeah," I admitted, and went on, "doesn't it strike you as a strange city, amigo?"

He was definitely annoyed now.

"Strange? Nonsense, amigo. To you everything is strange. You'll never succeed in life if you persist in thinking like this. You've got to know people and cities like the back of your hand so that you can exploit their weaknesses and take advantage of the opportunities. See what I mean? Now, why don't you try to get some sleep, amigo. We have a lot to do tomorrow. We'll strike oil, you'll see, amigo."

At that moment I discovered something in the straw.

I touched him on the shoulder.

"Amigo."

"What's the matter now, old buddy?"

"What do you think this could be? It's three or four centimeters long, roughly cylindrical in shape but thicker at the ends, and it's hard, smooth, and dry."

He didn't reply.

I persisted: "What do you think it is, amigo?"

"What I do think is that I won't be able to get any sleep."

I ignored his rudeness. "Couldn't it be a terminal phalanx, amigo?"

"What's a terminal phalanx?"

"A finger bone. The bone is quite dry, and fleshless."

He was silent. But he wasn't asleep; my guess was that he had become quite concerned.

"Here, hold it, amigo."

He hesitated, but then took the phalanx.

"So? What do you think?"

He didn't reply. I'll tell a few things about my friend: He's a young man; cool, thoughtful, shrewd. He believes he'll make a fortune by entering into some bold business deals.

He hasn't achieved his goal yet, but I think he's getting pretty close. We met by chance, for I'm a mere vagabond who is overcome by curiosity. We've been wandering from city to city: I look for food, old clothes, a woman once in a while; he sniffs out profitable deals. He believes that the right moment has finally arrived.

"No. Looks like a piece of bamboo to me. That's what it is, a small piece of bamboo." We've already found out about the bamboo groves around that city and we know that the construction of a huge bamboo-furniture factory is due to begin pretty soon. The construction of this factory is still a secret, but somehow he has managed to find out about it. A sharpie, that's my friend. "Throw this piece of rubbish away."

It seems to me that if bamboo is indeed so valuable, it's not fair to refer to it as rubbish. But my friend knows best and I discard the bone.

"What's the matter with this train, won't it ever pull out?" he asked.

My friend is getting impatient. He would like to set out on this trip right away: We'll be making our fortune in the next city. His plan of action is quite simple: The municipal government of the city where the bamboo grows has just issued public bonds. So far these bonds are worth nothing. But with the construction of the bamboo-furniture factory their value will rise tremendously.

Nobody in the next city knows about this factory yet: We'll buy the bonds there for peanuts and later resell them for ten times as much.

I'm still exploring the straw. "Friend ..."

"Yeah, what is it now?"

"Something long, smooth, and hard, with what feels like a head at the end ... what could it be?"

He hesitates and then breaks into laughter. "I've heard that gag somewhere before, but I can't think of a suitable repartee ..."

"It's not a gag, friend. It's something I'm holding in my hand."

"Ha, ha, ha!"

I fail to see what's so funny. "Couldn't it be a femur, friend?
A human femur."

Now he's no longer laughing. "Let me see it."

I hand him the femur. He is silent for a while.

"No. It looks like bamboo to me. Notice the strength and the
hardness of the bamboo that they grow in this city."

It is indeed quite surprising that nobody had thought before
of using this material to make furniture.

I still think it's a femur, but I say nothing to avoid getting
into an argument. I decide to change the subject. "Friend, wasn't
this train supposed to have left at nightfall? I find it strange that
it hasn't."

He rises to his feet: "It's really impossible to get any sleep here.
Okay, so the train hasn't left. So what? It's been delayed, that's
it. Don't trains often run behind schedule? To you everything is
strange. The bamboo is strange, this city is strange."

"I've heard stories about this city, amigo . . ."

"Stories, indeed, come on now!"

"I've heard that workers from all over the country are brought
here to work. They don't get paid for months."

"So? Don't they complain?"

"No, they disappear."

"Disappear? Only someone like you would believe something
like that. How in the world could a worker disappear just like
that?" I stood thinking about an explanation, but my friend pre-
vented me from replying: "Besides, we're investors; we're not
interested in money, not in its sources. Tomorrow we'll buy those
bonds . . ."

I was about to ask where we would get the capital to buy them,
but thought better of it: My friend is shrewd and must know
what he's doing. I was now amusing myself with something
vaguely reminiscent of a container with two cavities similar to
eye sockets. Interesting: I have never come across any bamboo
shaped like this.

"If this train leaves now, we'll be there at ten o'clock."

The train didn't leave. Suddenly, the door of the boxcar was
opened: There stood the police.

It looks as if we'll take this trip later on: Underneath the straw.

COMMUNICATION

ROBERTO GETS A PHONE CALL FROM HIS BROTHER MARCELO, WHO sounds distressed. The telephone connection is bad, and the only thing he can understand is the word "died."

"Who died? Who did you say died?" Roberto shouts. He is overcome with anxiety. Stammering, he repeats the same words.

The telephone connection, however, remains bad. Shouting, they tell each other to hang up and try again. Roberto puts the receiver down and waits impatiently for the phone to ring. Seconds, then minutes go by and the phone remains silent. It occurs to him that maybe he is expected to ring first.

"But what if I do," he says aloud to himself, "and Marcelo also thinks that he should ring first, and then if he does ring first, he'll get a busy signal. I'd better wait."

He keeps waiting. The telephone doesn't ring. More time goes by.

Then on the spur of the moment, he picks up the receiver and dials Marcelo's number; and just as he feared, he gets a busy signal.

He hangs up. He waits for a while, smoking and pacing back

and forth. Although he is convinced that he shouldn't dial again, he can't refrain himself from doing so. He hears the busy signal again.

Let's suppose that it takes a person one second to pick up the receiver; eight seconds to dial; two seconds to realize that the line at the other end is busy; fifteen to forty seconds to wait anxiously before dialing again. Let's figure out how long it will take Roberto to find Marcelo's phone free. And in addition, let's try to guess who has died.

HELLO! HELLO!

IRMA, A DEEPLY RELIGIOUS WOMAN, FALLS IN LOVE WITH HER CO-worker Teófilo, who is an atheist. Knowing that she will never be able to marry a man from whom she is kept apart by the barriers of her faith, she decides to move away from him, without ever letting him in on her feelings. She resigns from her job, moves to a distant neighborhood, and begins to lead a life of self-denial.

Periods of fasting and penance take place.

Her love, however, does not die, and Irma is tormented by yearnings. Every night she phones Teófilo.

"Hello!" he says.

Irma remains silent.

"Yes! Hello!"

Hearing the beloved voice, Irma quivers with pain and pleasure.

"Hello! Who's that? Answer me, will you?"

Irma cups her hand over the mouthpiece and quietly kisses her knuckles.

"Why don't you say something, you animal? Identify yourself."

Irma stifles a sob while abusive language pours out of the telephone. Finally, she hangs up.

This same routine goes on each night. Teófilo is beside himself with anger. He is so angry that he can't eat or sleep; he feels helpless.

On his friends' advice, he asks the police for help. An investigation reveals that the phone calls originate from Irma's telephone. Teófilo is asked to inform the police as soon as he gets the next mysterious call.

He does as he is told.

The policemen break into Irma's apartment and catch her still on the phone, as she is kissing the back of her thin hand. Moved by despair, she jumps out the window. Luckily, the building is not high and except for some abrasions, she is not injured. After receiving medical attention, she is taken to the police station.

Teófilo is called in.

He is shocked when he sees Irma surrounded by policemen. And to everybody's surprise, he shouts: "But I loved you, Irma! I loved you!"

"Begone, Satan," she replies, weeping.

The newsmen present at the scene understand her pain.

DR. SHYLOCK

It is said that in former days, Dr. Shylock used to be a notorious usurer. It is said that he lent a certain sum of money to a young man, demanding a pound of the debtor's own flesh as the only collateral. The debtor, sure that he would be able to repay the debt on time, acquiesced. However, it turned out that he was unable to do so, and Shylock, insensitive to the pleas from people of goodwill, demanded that the agreement between them be fulfilled.

Fortunately, the young man got a skillful lawyer to defend him. The lawyer pointed out to the court that the agreement clearly specified the word *flesh*, and not *blood*. The usurer could cut out a piece of *flesh* as long as he did not shed *blood*, not a drop of it. After this clever reasoning, there was nothing Shylock could do but beat a retreat amid widespread laughter.

This event took place a long time ago. Today Dr. Shylock is a famous surgeon.

True, he does have some idiosyncrasies. For instance, he demands that every single organ and tumor that he cuts out be carefully weighed: If the scales show that it weighs one pound, he laughs and claps his hands; if it weighs more, or less, he walks away dejectedly.

Nobody pays attention to this eccentricity of his. However, what everybody—professionals and laymen—does remark upon is Dr. Shylock's extraordinary skills: He has the ability to perform even the most complex operations without shedding a single drop of blood.